Jack Plays the Violin

by Jessica Schultz

illustrated by Luisa D'Augusta

SCHOLASTIC INC.

New York   Toronto   London   Auckland   Sydney
Mexico City   New Delhi   Hong Kong   Buenos Aires

Developed by Kirchoff/Wohlberg, Inc., in cooperation with Scholastic Inc.

Copyright © 2002 by Scholastic Inc.
All rights reserved.   Published by Scholastic Inc.   Printed in the U.S.A.
ISBN 0-439-35070-0
SCHOLASTIC and associated logos and designs are trademarks
and/or registered trademarks of Scholastic Inc.
10   40   09 08

Jack loved his violin. It was so shiny. He liked the way the bow looked. He liked the way it fit the case. He loved the sounds it made.

♫ 2 ♫

What Jack loved most was playing the violin. Jack played every day. His mom and dad never had to ask him.
He played for everyone. His dog Teddy watched. Teddy wagged his tail.

Another thing Jack loved was baseball. He was a good player. He was a great catcher. He played on a team.

🎵 4 🎵

One day, he had to leave the
game for a violin lesson.
   "The violin is not cool!" said Matt.
   "It's not," said Brett.
   "It's not," said Seth.
   Jack was sad. He wished his
friends would not make fun of him.

♩ 5 ♩

That night Jack talked with his dad.

"Matt said the violin is not cool!" cried Jack.

"Well, I play the violin," said Jack's dad. "Do you think I'm cool?"

"Yes!" said Jack. "You're great!

"So are you!" said his dad.

"People can be mean when there is something they don't understand," said Dad. "Someday they will understand."

Jack played a tune with his dad
that night.
"That was great!" said his mom.
"It was!" said his sister.
Teddy wagged his tail.
Jack felt a little better.

The next week there was a show at school. All the classes came. Matt, Brett and Seth sat in the first row. Jack's mom, dad, and sister came too. Teddy had to stay at home.

The music teacher announced Jack's name. He went up to the stage. He recited the name of the tune. He lifted his bow. He played a short tune.

He friends listened as he played.
"He's so good," whispered Seth.
"It looks like fun!" said Matt.
"I want to play!" said Brett.

After, everyone clapped. Jack smiled. He was happy with his playing.

"Great!" said his music teacher.

Jack saw his friends. They were clapping, too.

♪ 12 ♪

After school, the boys played baseball.

"I'm sorry I made fun of you," said Matt.

"Me too," said Brett.

"Me three," said Seth. "We must have hurt your feelings."

The next day, the music teacher came to their room. She asked if anyone wanted to take lessons.

"I want to," said Seth.

"I want to," said Matt.

"I want to," said Brett.

Jack was surprised.

Time went by. His friends learned to play a musical instrument.

Now Matt played the flute. Brett played the drums. Seth played the violin. Sometimes Seth and Jack played the same tune.

And they all still played baseball!